Burning
Reflection

By
Tim Mendees

ISBN: 9798699935819

First Edition 2020.
Cover design by Deidre J Owen © 2020 | deidrejowen.com
Source images from Pixabay.com.
Editing by Morgan Schafer at Mannison Press, LLC.
Visit mannisonpress.com.

A SPECIAL THANKS TO LINDA
AND EVERYONE ELSE WHO HAS HELPED ME OUT
ALONG THE WAY.

Aiden Conley grew up with the firm belief that his uncle Kenneth was a vampire. Upon reading the man's last will and testament, however, it became clear that it was something much more mundane...the man was as mad as a box of frogs. Kenneth had been a proudly confirmed bachelor and something of a dusty old recluse. Accordingly, as his only surviving relative, Aiden would inherit the man's assets. So far, so normal. It was the man's fear of mirrors that had Aiden scratching his balding pate in confusion.

One of the clauses in the will insisted that whoever received the property be given a dire warning about the mirrors. This warning came in the form of a tatty notebook stuffed with ill-fitting pages and tied up with darning wool. Aiden hadn't looked at it properly as yet, having merely glanced at a couple of the dog-eared pages; he was reserving that dubious pleasure for another day.

One of Aiden's earliest memories of Conley House, on the outskirts of the isolated village of Hollowhills, was his wild-eyed uncle bellowing at him for uncovering the mirror in the study. His father had later explained that Kenneth suffered from Spectrophobia, the fear of mirrors. It was partially due to this condition that Kenneth had abandoned his teaching post and retreated to the family pile where he remained in relative solitude until the day he died.

Every mirror and reflective surface in the large detached house overlooking Bodmin Moor was covered by a sheet or curtain and the silverware left to deliberately tarnish. He would only remove the coverings, to shave and whatnot, during daylight hours and never during the hours of darkness. Aiden never asked him what he was afraid of for fear of his fierce temper. During his teaching days, Kenneth had been given the unflattering nickname of "The Ogre of Truro." The children feared the man's wrath, and his dexterity with a cane, more than the Devil himself.

As Queen Victoria entered into the twilight of her reign, Kenneth Conley had cut himself off from the world and it appeared that, in conjunction to his pathological fear of reflective surfaces, that he was also suffering from agoraphobia. At least, this was the reason he gave for not attending his brother's funeral after his tragic death from consumption only a year before his own untimely demise. His small household staff catered to his every need and the local populous hadn't clapped their eyes on the man for over a year—not that any of them had missed the erratic old curmudgeon.

Aiden was thrilled to have inherited the old family pile as his current lodgings in the city of Truro were cramped, to say the least. He shared the modest townhouse with three other general practitioners so there was nary a surface that wasn't clogged to overflowing with documents, journals, and medical paraphernalia. One of the men had an unhealthy obsession with leeches that left the property smelling like a swamp on warm days. When the will was finally processed, and all legal matters attended to by the family solicitor, he wasted little time in packing up his meagre possessions and jumping on the first cart to Hollowhills.

Rain hammered the roof of the horse-drawn Hansome Cab as it rattled along the lonely lanes that threaded their way up into Bodmin Moor. The wind howled down the valley as the horses bravely soldiered on towards the village. It was just after three in the afternoon when they pulled up outside Conley House. Aiden jumped down from the cab and landed with both feet in the mud.

"Brilliant," he grumbled as he tried to wipe the worst of it off on the wheel. The driver got down from his perch and started to unload his luggage.

The house looked as though it had changed little in the decade or so since he last visited. The path was still choked with weeds and a veritable curtain of ivy clung stubbornly to the lime-washed edifice. Aiden took two of the heavier suitcases and navigated the crazy-paving path to the door. Placing the cases on the top step, he reached out and gave the rather unusual door knocker a good slam. The knocker was the only thing that he didn't recognise, it was in the shape of a strangely warped star with an eye in the centre. The knocking ring itself comprised the sclera, or white, of the eye and was embossed with an overhanging flame motif.

His knock echoed loudly in the dusty hall. He looked around self-consciously and was sure that he saw the curtains on the house down the road twitch furtively. After a moment of silence, he heard what sounded like a woman's footsteps tottering towards the door.

Following the clunk of the lock and the screech of tortured hinges, the door opened and Aiden was greeted by the pinched features of Mrs. Gittings, the housekeeper. She had been in his uncle's employ since he could remember. While the lines on her face had deepened into rough valleys, the expression hadn't changed one iota—she still looked like a bulldog sucking a thistle.

"Eh, Master Aiden," she said sourly. "I wasn't expecting you until tomorrow."

"Nice to see you too, Mrs. Gittings," Aiden quipped and removed his felt topper and brushed rain off the brim. "I had a cancellation this morning so I jumped on the opportunity, as it were, to get out here a day earlier and enjoy the weekend."

Aiden had arranged to go into practice with the local GP, Doctor Thomas Lester, starting the following Monday. Lester was getting on a bit and was grateful for the help.

A droplet of water splashed onto her sombre black dress. She eyed Aiden with contempt and clucked her tongue against the roof of her mouth before turning and beckoning him to follow. "This way, master Aiden." She always had a way of saying his name that made him feel like something she had scraped off her boot.

The coach driver placed the last of his luggage inside and beamed widely as Aiden gave him a generous tip. After closing the door, he followed Mrs. Gittings with two of his cases. "I'm exhausted from the journey, Mrs. Gittings, and would like to rest and wash up before dinner. What time will that be?"

"Cook usually has things ready for around six, sir," Gittings replied.

"Splendid. Then I shall not need your assistance any further, I know the way," Aiden said curtly. The foul weather and frosty reception he had received had frayed his temper somewhat and the housekeeper's sour demeanour was doing nothing to improve it.

Gittings harrumphed. "Very well, sir. Shall I have Kirsten call you when Cook is serving?"

"Yes, thank you, Mrs. Gittings, that would be splendid. Oh, and could you send an invitation to Doctor Lester to join me at said time?"

Mrs. Gittings sighed and pulled a pencil out of the tight grey weave on the top of her head and started scribbling on a crumpled piece of paper she fished from her pocket.

Aiden smiled and walked down the corridor towards the master bedroom. He had left instructions that it be cleared of his uncle's possessions and that they were to be moved to the study. As *he* was now the master of the house, it was only fitting that *he* had the master suite. Judging by the fact that he could feel the housekeeper's eyes burning holes in his back, Mrs. Gittings didn't agree.

Aiden had often mused as a child that there was something more than just an employer-employee relationship between those two and her demeanour and mourning dress would seem to suggest that he was correct in his assumption. One of the first things he was going to do once he settled in was rid himself of anything that reminded him of his dour uncle—including Mrs. Gittings.

He entered the room and was pleasantly surprised by its condition. The bed was made and the windows had been opened to allow it to be aired. The thick black curtains, however, remained tightly closed as per his uncle's instructions. He threw them wide in an act of defiance then placed his suitcases next to the mahogany wardrobe and kicked off his muddy boots. He had barely stretched out on the bed before he had drifted off into a fitful slumber.

♎︎⛢☌♏︎

The air in the study hung heavy and stifling. Aiden was a boy again, judging by his height. The sun was beating down outside but it was being kept at bay by the heavy curtains and barred windows. The door was normally locked but, on this occasion, Kenneth had neglected to do so. He took a few faltering steps across the threshold while making doubly sure that his uncle wasn't lurking behind the door brandishing his cane.

Only once had he felt his uncle's terrible wrath but that was enough to have scarred him for life. He couldn't remember what had earned him such treatment, but he was certain that he wasn't going to do anything that would drive him to repeat the punishment—or at least, not get caught.

The large desk sat to the rear of the room and was piled high with books and papers on mathematics and geometry; Kenneth had been a maths teacher, after all. Next to it stood a chalkboard covered in numbers. Aiden could see some of them clearly while others were hidden behind some kind of fog. It was as though his dream was only showing him what he could remember. For some reason, it seemed important to remember the numbers so he repeated them like a mantra:

"Twenty-two, 33, 55, 11..." Round and round. Always those numbers, always in that order. "Twenty-two, 33, 55, 11..."

As he intoned the numbers, Aiden found himself drawn to the mirror that hung above the fireplace. It was covered with a black velvet cloth that had been nibbled by moths. To this day he didn't know why he had uncovered it. He had never so much as glanced at the others around the house. Now he understood why.

The mirror was shaking. Almost imperceptibly, but enough to make the velvet sway. Its vibration was coupled with a sound akin to the roar of a fire. It was very faint, but it brought to mind a damp log being tossed on the fire and smouldering as it dried out.

Aiden dragged his uncle's footstool across to the hearth and stood on it. Even with its assistance, he was too short to reach the velvet drape. He stood on tiptoes and stretched out his hand towards it. The cloth was warm to the touch and as he dragged it down the reflective glass of the mirror, it almost seemed to hiss.

"What are you doing, boy!"

Aiden snapped his neck around and toppled from the stool as his uncle burst into the room. The door slammed into the wall, smashing a dent into the plaster where the knob struck. Kenneth's eyes were ablaze with fury and something he hadn't noticed at the time—fear.

"I'm sorry, Uncle," Aiden babbled as the towering figure stormed across the room in his direction. "I thought there was something behind it."

Aiden scrambled backwards away from his uncle. The fire in his eyes seemed to grow in intensity as he neared the mirror. He was so angry that it appeared that smoke was literally coming out of his ears.

In fact, his whole body was smouldering.

"What have you done?" Kenneth growled furiously, spitting sparks and embers that twisted to the carpet. "Meddlesome child!"

Aiden let out a little cry of fear as his back connected with one of the overloaded bookcases—he had run out of room to flee. Kenneth stretched out his smoking hands for Aiden's face, sparks dancing between his trembling fingers. The heat was unbearable. The fact that his uncle looked as though he was going to place them on his cheeks filled him with dread, anticipating agonising pain. Sweat beaded up on Aiden's brow as he whimpered and cried.

"What the devil is going on in here?"

Kenneth stopped at the sound of Aiden's father Jonathan's raised voice. His hands abruptly changed course and snatched the velvet drape off the hearth. In a second he had replaced it and his temperature instantly returned to normal. His temper, however, was still irretrievably lost.

"Go downstairs, Aiden," his father had snarled as he glared a hole through his brother. "I'll deal with you in a minute."

Aiden hurried from the room still repeating the numbers, though they now came out in a splutter of sniffles and saliva. "Twenty-two, 33, 55, 11..."

He turned as he left the room and the door slammed loudly behind him. What he heard next could only be described as a furious row. His father was warning Kenneth not to lay his hands on Aiden; last time had been more than enough. He was his child, so he would dole out the punishments and if he so much as touched him again then he would deliver a sound thrashing to his elder sibling.

As he backed away from the stout oak door, unnerved by his father's rage, he suddenly became aware of two things: One, all the candles on the landing were lit despite it being mid-morning. And two, someone was standing right behind him.

"He's coming!" Mrs. Gittings chuckled through a rictus grin as she reached out with burning hands...

Aiden screamed.

♎ℇℨℭᚾ

"Eleven!"

Aiden sat up in his bed pouring with sweat. It took a few seconds to realise that it had been a dream, it had been so vivid.

His body temperature had rocketed and his pulse raced. He rolled off the bed and into the washroom where he splashed his face with water that, presumably, Kirsten had earlier drawn from the well. He didn't know whether it had been there when he first nodded off but he was damn glad of it being there.

He hadn't even thought of that day never mind dreamt about it for decades. It was one of those awful childhood memories that had been mercifully buried under years of happy ones. He looked up from the basin and scowled. The shaving mirror was covered with a dusty curtain of black fabric.

"Damn nonsense," Aiden spat as he tore away the cover, scrunched it up and used it to buff the glass. "Well, I will not be governed by the wishes of a dead lunatic!" He tossed the fabric into the wastepaper basket and dried his hands on an old towel that was hanging by the door.

The cold water had done the trick and the terror had quickly receded from his mind. While he had been sleeping, the weather had brightened significantly. His father had often said that the Cornish weather was as changeable as a politician's promises. Bright sunlight and a fresh salty breeze did wonders for his head and quickly blew out the cobwebs.

A quick glance at his fob-watch told him that it was half-past five and that dinner would be served soon so he set about making himself presentable. It was while he was moving one of his cases to the stout wooden dresser that he spotted a hastily scrawled note that had been slipped under the door. It informed him in cursive script that evidently belonged to Kirsten, judging by the K on the bottom, that Doctor Lester would indeed be joining him for a spot of dinner.

"Good," he muttered to himself. "I could do with his professional opinion of this." He tapped Kenneth's ratty notebook with the flat of his palm. He had looked over a couple of pages on the journey and had deduced that, at the time of its writing, his uncle had been as mad as a bag of badgers. It never hurt to get a second opinion. Also, he was still perplexed as to what had finally polished the old buzzard off. The death certificate had cryptically listed it as: "natural causes." He knew only too well how much could be held under that particular umbrella.

Presently, there came a knock at his door. "Hello?" he called in response.

"Beggin' yer pardon, sir," a female voice answered. "But Mrs. Gittings told me to inform you that cook will be serving dinner in half an hour and that Doctor Lester is waiting for you in the drawing room."

Aiden opened the door and was greeted by the pleasant open features of a young maid. "Ah, yes. Kirsten is it?"

"Yes, sir." She smiled and did a clumsy attempt at a curtsy.

"Aiden, please." He returned the smile. "Tell the old bat that I'll be right down."

Kirsten stifled a giggle. "Yes, Aiden, right away."

Aiden closed the door before putting on his tie and slipping on his evening jacket. With the notebook safely tucked into one of his pockets, he left the room. The master bedroom was at the far end of the landing. Despite the fact that it was the middle of summer and there would be daylight for at least another two to three hours, the house was enveloped in shadow.

He paused in his journey downstairs as he passed one of the iron candle sconces that had been built into the wooden paneling. The dream flashed before his eyes once more. He was sure that they hadn't been lit when he went into the study but when he came out... Aiden shuddered. It was involuntary, like someone with multiple legs was tap dancing on his grave. It took a second or two for it to register that what he was feeling was fear, an overwhelming feeling of dread inexplicable to his rational mind.

Taking a deep breath, Aiden chided himself for his foolishness. It was just a dream, after all. He knew enough about the workings of the human subconscious to know that it was a distorted memory of a traumatic episode, an embellishment of the facts. Once his hands had stopped trembling, the fear was replaced by another emotion—anger.

"Damn you, Kenneth," he hissed under his breath and marched to the window at the end of the corridor. "...And damn your curtains!" With an overwhelming feeling of catharsis, Aiden tore the heavy curtain from the railing and tossed it into the corner in ignominy. Bright sunlight streaked through the grimy window, its diffused rays casting prismatic rainbows on the hardwood flooring.

"There. That's better." Aiden straightened his tie and smoothed his moustache with his thumb and forefinger.

Upon turning around, he was startled to find himself face-to-hatchet-face with Mrs. Gittings. Aiden let out a startled yelp as the aged housekeeper glared at the exposed window with a look of fury.

"What the devil are you doing?" she spat in a venomous manner. "Master Kenneth—"

Before she could fully launch into her timeworn speech, Aiden stopped her short with a finger to his lips and a sibilant *shush*. He could see the anger in the woman's eyes as he finished the sentence for her. "Master Kenneth is dead. I will not live in darkness like a flaming mushroom because of some lunatic whim of a dead relative. I am the master of this house now, Mrs. Gittings, and you would do well to remember that!"

That felt good. He had been dying to put the haughty harridan in her place ever since he was a child. She had always been the same, lurking around the house spitting poison like a disgruntled puff adder. "Now, how many staff are currently in residence?"

Gittings took a deep breath to compose herself before responding. Aiden had never seen her rendered speechless before, she was always quick with a sharp reply. "Five. Apart from myself, there is Kirsten, Mary the cook, Tom the stable boy, and Jack the odd-job man. Kirsten and I live in the house, while Tom and Jack live in the small cottage next to the stables. Mary lives in the village and leaves after mealtimes." She ended her speech with another uneasy glance at the window. Was that fear he could see in her slate-grey eyes?

"Marvelous," Aiden smiled thinly. "I can't imagine that Tom and Jack are busy with anything at the moment. Have them wash the windows. We will not be living like moles for another minute." With that, he left Mrs. Gittings with her mouth agape before she could argue. It felt good to finally stand up to the domineering housekeeper. It was nice to finally banish some childhood demons. He walked on past the staircase to the opposite end of the corridor and repeated his actions with the other window. He was almost certain that he heard Gittings squeak in outrage and smiled.

The affronted housekeeper scuttled down the stairs ahead of him at a pace he would never have imagined. She could have given Olympic sprinters a good run for their money. She swept through the vestibule and into the scullery, slamming the door behind her. This time, Aiden grinned.

Aiden took his time walking down the stairs in order to examine the portraits of Conleys throughout history. He had never known who this rogues gallery represented but the one in the powdered wig always made him chuckle. It was a mystery to him why people had ever worn the frightful things. Still, the family resemblance was uncanny.

Kirsten was standing at the entrance to the drawing room trying to keep a straight face when Aiden reached the bottom of the stairs. Clearly, she had witnessed the confrontation on the landing. Aiden could well imagine what purgatory it must have been for the poor youngster, having Gittings as her superior and Kenneth as her master. A prolonged stay in Bedlam would probably have been preferable.

"Kirsten, are the cellars as well-stocked as ever?" Aiden asked while he buffed his wire-rim spectacles on his sleeve.

"Yes, master Aiden. Your uncle was a connoisseur," she replied politely.

"That's one word for it. Very good, could you get us a bottle of red? Something fruity, maybe a Claret?"

"Right away. I'll ask Cook what she would recommend having with the meal. It's venison."

"Ooh, splendid!" Aiden grinned, his digestive juices flowing at the thought. "One of my favourites."

Kirsten curtsied and headed towards the kitchen. Aiden opened the door to the drawing room and greeted his guest. "Lester, my good man. So glad of you to come."

The drawing room was a lavish affair with comfortable leather couches and wingback chairs. The walls were lined with beautifully bound books and curios from generations of Conley. Lester was over in the far corner perusing a well-out-of-date medical encyclopedia. "Nonsense," he beamed. "I can't resist Mary's cooking and I have missed it of late. I've had no cause to drop in since your uncle's passing. I confess that I used to time my visits to coincide with lunch in the hope I would be allowed to stay. Mrs. Lester, god rest her soul, was never much of one for the culinary arts." He closed the book and a plume of dust shot up from the pages.

"Well, you are always welcome to join me. As you know, I have never married and sometimes crave intelligent conversation." Aiden stopped talking and his brow creased in irritation. "Excuse me one moment," he said as he navigated the furniture and approached the large bay window. The curtain runners screeched and complained as he forced the black fabric aside to reveal the warm glow of the evening sun over a neatly tended rose bush. "There, that's better."

Lester chuckled. "A great improvement. In all my time as Kenneth's doctor, I have never once seen that curtain open. I was starting to wonder if there really was a window and not just a brick wall."

"Well, I'm not having it any longer. It's enough to drive a person mad being kept in the dark like some kind of ghoul."

"Yes, well..." Lester gave a discreet cough. "Your uncle had his quirks."

"Indeed. That's one of the reasons I asked you to join me, actually. I understand that it was you who delivered the death certificate? I wondered if you could clarify what the cause of death was?"

Lester nodded sombrely. "I will do the best that I can. I confess to being somewhat perplexed by the whole affair myself. You see, he was found in the study, where he had practically isolated himself for the last few weeks of his life, appearing to have died from some kind of seizure. He had been somewhat manic leading up to the end and was in what I would describe as a profoundly nervous state. I had prescribed him a tincture of laudanum to soothe his nerves but, alas, it seemed to help none. I examined his body myself and performed an autopsy, but I was at a loss to find any factor that might have contributed to his attack.

"There was no evidence of blood or lesions on the brain so I could rule out apoplexy with confidence. Similarly, his heart and lungs were sound. In short, your uncle was as solid as an oak. I could only surmise that he suffered sudden heart failure due to his nervous state." Lester fussed with his tie as he spoke. Clearly, not knowing was causing him some professional discomfort.

"So, you think he died of fright?" The hairs on the back of Aiden's neck stood up.

"Precisely. As I say, he had gotten himself whipped into a lather recently and this was the root cause of his demise."

"Was there anything else of note?"

Lester thought for a minute. "Only his clothes," he mused. "They were completely soaked with sweat. Almost like a fever but without any other viral evidence."

The sentence hung heavy over Aiden's head. His mind flashed back to that awful dream. His uncle had been incredibly hot, almost burning. The coincidence punched him in the gut like a prizefighter.

Knock, knock.

The sudden rap at the door brought him around in an instant. "Enter."

Kirsten opened the door and gestured to the dining room across the hall. "Dinner is served, sirs. I have uncorked the wine and poured you both a glass."

"Smashing!" Lester beamed.

"Thank you, Kirsten. We will be along straight away."

"You must be famished after your journey," Lester inquired as the two men left the drawing room.

"Indeed I am," Aiden confessed. Though his appetite had diminished somewhat since hearing about his uncle's sweat-soaked clothing and mysterious death.

ᛟᛒᚷᛚ

The conversation had been confined to less troubling topics while both men tucked into their meals. Mary had outdone herself, the meat was tender, the potatoes crisp with fluffy centres and the gravy was divine. Kirsten's choice of wine had complemented the meat fabulously and both men had a rosy glow.

During the meal, a lad of around nineteen, Tom presumably, had washed the two large windows on the north wall. He had doffed his cap at them and carried out his task with gusto. Aiden thought that the lad must have been appreciating the winds of change that were blowing through Conley House.

After the meal was consumed, Lester and Aiden retired to the drawing room for brandy and cigars. Once Kirsten had supplied two snifters and the decanter, they had fixed themselves drinks and sank into the luxurious seating. After briefly discussing surgery matters ahead of his start on Monday, Aiden decided to broach the subject of the notebook. He took it out of his pocket and handed it to Doctor Lester.

"Here, see what you make of this," he said with a cocked eyebrow.

As Lester was about to ask what it was he was looking at, he was startled by a high-pitched voice from behind them. "Master Aiden!" Mrs. Gittings wailed shrilly. "I don't think it proper that you share Master Kenneth's private notes with all and sundry!"

Aiden was rendered momentarily speechless by her intrusion. Neither man had known she was there. Lester, however, bristled at her last comment. "All and sundry? I'll have you know—"

"Please, Doctor Lester. Let *me* deal with my *impertinent* staff." He pronounced every syllable for maximum effect. "Now, look here, Gittings. I have had almost all I can take of your attitude. Doctor Lester was my uncle's practitioner, so he is well aware of his *quirks.* It is also none of your business to whom I show things that have been left to me by law."

"But, Master Aiden, please—"

"No!" Aiden boomed. "That will be all, Mrs. Gittings. Leave us!"

Suitably cowed, Gittings fled from the room. Lester was suitably impressed by Aiden's show of dominance over the uppity housekeeper. "Well, blow me down. I've never known anyone talk to her like that. Even Kenneth seemed afraid of her razor-tongued wrath."

"Well, I won't stand for it any longer. You know she tried to stop me from opening the damn curtains earlier? Any more of her nonsense and she can pack her bags and leave." His spleen suitably vented, Aiden took a hearty glug of brandy and relaxed. He motioned for Lester to look at the notebook. "So, what do you think?"

Lester scratched his head and his mighty muttonchops as he flicked through the pages. They started out with several seemingly random numbers followed by several pages of odd geometric designs. When he reached the meat of the notes, he had to pause and look at Aiden with an expression of shock. "I knew he had some *outré* thoughts, but this..."

"I know." Aiden nodded and took another sip of brandy.

Lester started to read snatches of the notes aloud: "'*Mirrors hold the key. I first thought that I was hallucinating but my calculations have proved to be effective in opening a link to Fomalhaut...*' Fomalhaut?"

Aiden shrugged. "Your guess is as good as mine."

The doctor flipped forward a couple of pages and continued, "'*Yes! Mirrors are the key to it all. Not just the physical reflection but the concept of reflected space. Mirror hours hold significance in numerology.*'" He flipped some more pages growing paler as he did. "'*It is written by Prinn, d'Erlette and Goterrez that he can be drawn from Fomalhaut...*'" Lester stopped and looked at Aiden. "I'm sorry to say this, but I think your uncle was certifiable."

Aiden agreed, but something Lester had just read distracted his attention. "Hold on, what was the second name he mentioned? I think I've seen it somewhere before."

"d'Erlette?" Lester replied after scrutinising the notes.

"That's it. I've seen that name before."

"So have I," Lester spoke in dire tones. "It's a book in your uncle's study. It's written by one Francois-Honore Balfour the Comte d'Erlette. Your uncle was reading it the day he died. It was on the desk in front of him. In fact, his head was resting on it." He paused, wetting his lips with a sip of brandy before continuing. "It's called Cultes Des Gou—"

A piercing shriek echoed around the house, stopping Lester in his tracks.

"What the hell was that?" Aiden cried in alarm.

As the two men got to their feet, Kirsten burst into the room without any preamble. "Oh, sirs, come quick! It's Tom. He's had an accident." Without waiting for a response, she raced from the room and out the front door. The two men followed.

♎⛢♅♇

Tom was lying on his back with a ladder across his legs directly under the landing window. He had cracked his head on the paving and appeared to be unconscious. Jack, the old odd-job man was slapping the back of his hand and trying to bring him round.

"What happened?" Aiden panted. As the younger and considerably lighter of the two doctors, he was first on the scene with Kirsten.

"I dunno fer sure, sir," Jack mumbled in his thick Cornish burr. "I wus talkin' to miss Kirsten 'ere over by the stables when we 'eard one 'ell of a shout. Anyway, we ran over just in time to see poor Tom 'ere fall backwards off the ladder."

"Move aside, Jack," Aiden said calmly. "Kirsten, run up to my room and fetch my medical bag. It's on the table by the window." While she ran off to do as he asked, Aiden loosened Tom's collar and started to examine him. Lester had arrived by this point and had removed his jacket to place under the injured man's head.

"You say he screamed and *then* fell?" Aiden asked Jack.

The grizzled old-timer rubbed his whiskery chin then answered, "Aye. It were a few seconds afore 'e fell. Screamed like the devil 'imself had shown up, 'e did."

Aiden glanced up at the window just for a second. The first thing he noticed was the flare of the sinking sun on the glass. It was dazzling to the naked eye and he winced as it burned his retinas. He was averting his eyes when he saw movement behind the flare. It was dim and shadowy as though something or someone were moving behind the window. He shielded his eyes with his hand and squinted at the shape. The flare and the decades of grime had conspired to give it an unnatural, formless aspect. Maybe it was just a trick of the light?

"Aiden," Lester said again. Apparently, he had been speaking while Aiden had been distracted.

"Yes...sorry. What is it?" Aiden looked at Lester and had to fight against the urge to glance up at the window again. In the end, he failed and raised his head. The shadow had gone and the glare had receded as a low black cloud passed overhead.

"I said, I think we should get him to the surgery. He's got a nasty wound on his head that will require stitches."

"I agree." Aiden said, nodding. "Jack, get the cart ready, will you? We can lay him down in the back."

Jack grunted and limped off towards the stables just as Kirsten came racing towards them carrying Aiden's medical bag. "Here you go, master Aiden."

He took the bag and opened it. "Thank you, Kirsten. Could you draw some water from the well?"

"At once, sir." She barely paused for breath before racing off on another errand. She was certainly earning her meagre wages that day.

The two doctors stemmed the bleeding and checked Tom's skull for any noticeable damage. Luckily, the laceration was the only readily identifiable wound to his head. Aiden took out a bottle of smelling salts and wafted it under the boy's nose. After a couple of sniffs, Tom coughed and his eyelids flickered open. His eyes were rolled into the back of his head revealing two white orbs.

"Don't let it get me!" Tom screamed hysterically as his hands shot up defensively.

"Tom, calm down. You are going to be okay. It's me, Doctor Lester."

After another second or two, his eyes rolled back to normal and the stable boy blinked in confusion. "Doctor Lester? Master Conley? Wh-...What happened?"

"Relax," Aiden said calmly with a smile. His bedside manner had always been impeccable. "You are all right now. You've just had a bit of an accident, that's all. Nothing is going to hurt you." What made him say *nothing* instead of *nobody* is a question that he struggled to answer. "We are going to take you to Doctor Lester's surgery to get you some stitches."

"Accident?" Tom's brow creased as he struggled to remember. "Yes, I fell off the ladder... There was a flash... Then a face! A face at the window!"

"Whose face, Tom?" Aiden asked with mounting concern and suspicion.

"Dunno," Tom muttered. His voice was slurred, indicating that he had a serious concussion. "It was old and twisted. I couldn't make it out because of the sun in my eyes. Furious, it was. Those eyes..."

"Never mind about that now," Lester purred. "You need to try to stay calm. Aside from your head, is there any other pain?"

Tom sniggered, then winced in pain. "Yeah, my arse hurts, doctor. It ain't nice to kick a man when he's down."

Aiden struggled to stifle a laugh. "It's likely that you have a bruised tailbone. It seems that your sense of humour hasn't been affected."

"Well, you have to laugh, don't you? If you didn't laugh at times like this, you'd be a right miserable bugger." He stretched out a welcoming hand to Aiden. "Tom Stevens, pleased to meet you, master Conley. I run the stables and look after your horse, Ludwig."

Aiden shook his hand. "Pleased to meet you, Tom. And, please, call me Aiden. Master Conley was my uncle." Releasing his hand, Aiden looked over at the roan horse that Jack was leading from the stables. "What a magnificent beast. Is he a Cleveland Bay? With a name like Ludwig, I was expecting a German breed."

Tom chuckled, giving him another cause to wince. "Aye, you're right. It's a Cleveland Bay, all right. What's more, *he* is a *she.*"

Aiden held his hands up in amused confusion. "Then, why the devil did my uncle name an English nag Ludwig?"

"No idea. He named her after some writer fellow, isn't that right, Jack?"

Jack was in earshot now and nodded. "Aye, after some feller called Prinn. I told 'im she were a lady, but 'e were set on the name. So, we 'ave a mare called Ludwig. Yer uncle were a willful man, sir, as I'm sure ye know. Nowt were changin' 'is mind once it were set on summat."

"That's true."

"Master Aiden, here's the water," Kirsten said as she plonked the bucket down next to the bag. Aiden thanked her and took a wad of gauze from his bag and wetted it in the cool well water. Tom winced yet again as Aiden cleaned his wound. With help from the two doctors, Tom was able to sit up and was manoeuvred onto the cart.

"I can take care of him from here, Aiden. I'll have him patched up and put to bed in a couple of hours. You must be exhausted." Lester smiled.

"I am." But, despite his words, he wasn't tired. His troubled mind was racing at a hundred miles per hour. "As long as you are sure?"

Lester assured him that he and Tom would be fine and that the best thing he could do at that moment was to get some rest. Aiden nodded and watched as Jack led the oddly named nag by the nose, trundling Tom and Lester in the flatbed cart behind them.

Aiden turned to Kirsten. "Where's Gittings?"

"I don't know, sir. I haven't seen her since she helped serve dinner."

"Hmm." Suspicion as to the identity of the spectral figure in the window was growing in Aiden's mind. "Very well. Thank you for your help. You may as well take the rest of the night off. I will be fine."

"Thank you, master Aiden." Her face lit up. After all of her running about, her feet were killing her. An early night was just the ticket. She didn't have to be told twice and hurried off towards the front door, nearly colliding with Mrs. Gittings who had just appeared from around the corner wearing a foul expression.

Aiden walked up to the housekeeper. "Where have you been?" he asked in measured tones.

"Attending to my duties, master Aiden," she replied primly. "What's all this fuss, anyway?"

"This *fuss,* as you put it, was poor Tom being startled off his ladder. The poor fellow nearly broke his neck."

Gittings adopted a haughty expression. "I knew no good would come of messing around with the windows. Master Kenneth—"

Aiden held up his hand. "Enough." He looked Gittings in the eyes. "*Someone* scared him out of his wits."

Gittings didn't blink. "Well, I'm sure that I don't know who could have done such a thing."

The corner of Aiden's mouth twisted into a wry smirk, tipping his sandy moustache diagonally across his face. "Yes...I bet you don't." He sharply turned from her and walked into the house leaving Gittings simmering on the path.

One thing was certain at that moment: if looks could indeed kill, the one that Gittings gave Aiden as he walked away would have had him on the mortuary slab before you could say, "disgruntled."

♀ℬℨΠ

Once back inside Conley House, Aiden retrieved his uncle's notebook along with the decanter containing the brandy and his glass then retired to the study. It was around a quarter to eight by this point and he had barked at Mrs. Gittings as he passed her in the hall that he was not to be disturbed under any circumstances until Tom returned. Jack and Tom were still with Doctor Lester and Kirsten had retired to her chamber. The only noise in the grand old house beside the ponderous ticking of the grandfather clock were the sounds of Mary washing the dishes in the kitchen at the rear. After a little while he heard her leave via the back door. Gittings distractedly busied herself in the drawing room with a duster.

Aiden had taken great pleasure in uncovering mirrors as he passed them on his way to the study on the upper floor. It had struck him as distinctly curious that a man with a pathological fear of reflective surfaces would persist in keeping so many mirrors. Surely, it would have been beneficial to his mental state to have gotten rid of as many mirrors as possible? Aiden ruminated that perhaps they were worth a bob or two and that's why he kept them. Still, it was yet another mystery for him to puzzle over.

Stepping into the former stronghold of his crazed relative was another shock to the senses. Since that one time that he sneaked into the study as a child, his uncle's monomania had seemingly escalated beyond all control. There were now several chalkboards all covered in a scrawl of numbers, and piles of papers and dusty old tomes littered the floor. The only vaguely ordered space was the desk itself. The papers and notes were in neat piles and space was left for books.

Aiden took the notebook from his pocket and placed it onto the desk. He poured himself a large measure and sat in his uncle's wingback chair. It wasn't very comfortable as chairs go as his uncle's increasingly large frame had bent it all out of proportion. It was moulded to Kenneth's shape. It was lucky that he had the brandy to take the edge off his discomfort.

"Twenty-two, 33, 55, 11," Aiden said softly, recalling his dream, as he looked at the chalkboard next to the desk. The numbers were still there. They had been gone over in fresh chalk so many times that the numbers were bold and bloated. The number 33 had been circled with such fervour that it looked like the chalk had snapped under the pressure of Kenneth's paw.

"Thirty-three?" Aiden took a sip of brandy and leaned back in the chair. "What's so dashed important about the number 33?" Adjacent to the number 33 was another number, 2112. It was now that he noticed that all of the other numbers he remembered had longer numbers next to them: 22 was next to 2002, 55 was next to 2332, and 11 was next to 110.

Aiden scratched his chin and absently plucked the top leaf from a stack of papers. It was blank except for a number of words listed from top to bottom, thus:

Ambition–Accomplishment–Depression– Self Destruction

Communication–Persuasion

Change–Struggle–Aggression

Betrayal

The words Communication and Persuasion were similarly ringed in a frantic whirl of ink. He placed the paper down on the desk and started to pick books at random from the pile nearest to the desk. Amongst some well out-of-date studies on anthropology and the dubious works of occultists such as Blavatsky, were several books on the subject of numerology. The topmost tome was well-thumbed and dog-eared. What's more, Kenneth had scribbled many notes and had marked certain pages with them.

Opening the book at the first marker, Aiden gasped at the illegible scrawl that his uncle's once neat hand had degenerated into. It was hard to credit that it was Kenneth's writing at all. It was a page of rambling on the subject of the number 22. "'*Twenty-two is the key to accomplishment*...'" Aiden read as best he could. "'*In order to release...something... one must be sure that ambition doesn't lead to self-destruction*...'" He stopped and held the paper with the words on it next to the chalkboard.

"Twenty-two means ambition, accomplishment, depression, and self-destruction. So that would mean that 33 means communication and persuasion. But what of the number next to it? And why is it so damned important?" He scrutinised the board for several minutes before clapping the book shut with a huff and placing it back onto the pile. "Mad as a blasted badger," he sighed. "What the hell was he working on?"

The light from the open curtains was failing now so he struck a Lucifer and lit the candle on the desk. It flickered for a second as an otherwise imperceptible breeze came from one of the corners. Leaning back in the chair once more and swirling the brandy around the glass, Aiden looked up at the mirror over the fireplace. It was still covered in the same black velvet drape as that terrible day all those years ago.

"Damn you, Uncle Kenneth...damn you to the fiery pits of hell," he said, raising his glass to the mirror in an act of ironic defiance. Once he had taken a sip, the burn of the liquid quickly turned into a burning urge to rip down the drape once and for all. He got out of the chair, placed the glass on a wooden coaster advertising a local brewery and picked his way through the stacks of books and paper.

Stopping in front of the mirror, Aiden was suddenly filled with an inexplicable feeling. It wasn't quite fear, it was more like dread anticipation. As he reached out his left hand towards the fabric, the tips of his fingers began to tingle. The feeling raced down his arm and fluttered down his spine making him shiver. Clenching his fist to banish the sensation, Aiden moved his hand the final few inches to the mirror.

Ding, ding, ding!

"Bloody hell!" Aiden leapt into the air as the grandfather clock struck eight. He had been so wrapped up in the moment that the sudden appearance of reality scared the life out of him. Chuckling to himself, Aiden took a deep breath. "What the hell is wrong with you?" he thought aloud. "It's just a ruddy mirror. A pane of reflective glass, nothing more. If you're not careful, you will go as batty as that old fool Gittings." The thought of Mrs. Gittings made his blood boil. He had become increasingly convinced that she was behind poor Tom's tumble off the ladder.

Galvanised by his anger, Aiden tore the drape away from the mirror and threw it into the fireplace where it settled on a stack of kindling ready for the touch of a match. "There!" he panted in triumph and placed his hands on his hips.

The unveiling came as a complete anticlimax. All his life, this wretched mirror had hung over his head like the sword of Damocles. It represented all of his childhood fears and anxieties. A small part of him had been expecting some kind of fanfare, some kind of catharsis. But, in the end, it was just a mirror and a pretty boring one at that.

Time and tarnish had transformed the once-gleaming silver frame into something that wouldn't look out of place in a haunted house. A smile fluttered across his lips as a cruel idea passed into his head. He knew exactly who he was going to put to work on reviving the piece—Mrs. Gittings. *I'll give her a reason to hate bloody mirrors,* he thought to himself spitefully.

Taking a handkerchief from his top pocket, Aiden breathed on the mirror and gave it a good buffing. Soon, the mist had cleared and he could see himself at last. The flickering light from the candle reflected off the mirror gave him a cadaverous appearance. His eyes appeared sunken and his cheeks sallow. "Blimey, you need a good night's sleep," he told his reflection.

As he brushed his moustache with his fingers, his eyes were drawn to the candle. The blooming effect of the glass had magnified the small flame to the size of a tennis ball. Aiden marveled at the trails and tendrils that danced around its edges.

All sounds from the house faded except the hollow tick-tock of the grandfather clock. After a moment, the flame seemed to flicker to the steady rhythm. It went right on every *tick* and left on every *tock*.

The effect was hypnotic. Aiden was incapable of looking away and found himself being drawn deeper and deeper into the reflection. The still silver portions of the flame glittered and sparkled around the edges, giving it an almost magical aspect. It looked like some kind of shimmering door or window...as though he was gazing at another world.

Two minutes had passed since the eight o'clock chime and for the last of those, Aiden had been mesmerised. As he gazed into the mirror, unblinking, the flame grew swollen and bulbous. It seemed to be swelling and pulsing. The wispy fronds of flame started to radiate further and further outwards from its centre. The rest of the room flickered with an undulating shadow that played on the walls like they were alive; thick and tentacle-like, they spread and grew, devouring what remained of the light.

The ticking of the clock grew in rapidity as time started to race. Aiden's eyes swam and bobbed with the dance of the now enormous flame. His mouth had dried and his pulse quickened. He couldn't take his eyes off the reflection of the flame. It had bloated up so greatly that it now filled the glass. Aiden's eyes stung and watered as the light seared them with its brilliance. Sweat started to pour in rivulets from his receding hairline as the temperature rose by degrees.

Aiden's breathing started to come in ragged gasps in time to the now speeding clock. The flame pulsed and swirled. Strangely sibilant whisperings started to sneak into his head. It was as though something inside his head was speaking. There was no external sound, just a strangely internal one. His body temperature had risen to such heights that his extremities felt like they were ablaze. He could feel himself burning up. Being consumed in an unholy conflagration. He was reaching the point where his brain would begin to boil in its own cerebral fluid, when—

Knock, knock, knock!

The sudden loud knock on the door brought the room back into focus. Aiden gasped and pitched forward, grabbing the mantlepiece for support as he screwed his eyes up tightly. The heat in the room quickly dispersed and the sweat on his brow felt like droplets of ice.

"Master Aiden, sir," a rough voice called after another three firm knocks. "Is everythin' all right, sir?"

Aiden rubbed his eyes until he could see again and sucked in some air before answering. "Yes, Jack...I'm fine. Come in."

Jack opened the door and looked around the room. His eyes took in the piles of books, the mirror, and Aiden's disheveled appearance. He looked like death warmed up. Even to a casual observer, it was clear that he had just been through some kind of trauma. "Are ye sure, yer alright, sir? If ye don't mind me sayin, ye look like hell, sir."

Aiden smiled. He had always liked Jack; he had been around since his grandfather's time and had always been something of a rascal. Aiden greedily sucked in oxygen, every breath making him feel slightly more human. "just felt a bit lightheaded, that's all. Nothing to worry about." Aiden wasn't sure who he was trying to convince, Jack or himself. Finally composing himself, he stepped away from the fireplace and turned to Jack. "So, how's Tom?"

"That's what I came to tell ye. Tom's 'ome. Doctor Lester is makin' sure 'e gets comfortable. Lester were wonderin' if ye had a moment."

"Certainly," Aiden said as enthusiastically as he could muster. "you go on ahead. I'll be over in a moment."

"Right you are, sir." Jack left the room leaving the door ajar.

Once Jack had gone, Aiden's facade dropped like a stone and he doubled over with his palms on the desk panting with shock. "What the hell just happened?" he managed to ask between ragged gasps. Lifting his right hand, he reached over and scooped up the brandy and knocked the remainder of the liquid back in one mighty gulp. Aiden winced and spluttered then took a deep breath and counted to ten. "Eleven?" he whispered as he reached the end.

The candle flame fluttered with every deep exhalation but was back to normal. The human mind has a tremendous knack for rationalisation in the face of the inexplicable and Aiden's mind told him that what had just transpired was merely a combination of a common reflective phenomenon, his tired mental state, and all the booze he had been imbibing—the nonsense in his uncle's notes couldn't have helped any either.

A couple of minutes passed before his mind suddenly snapped back into place. It was as though something had just released it from a suffocating embrace. The clouds parted in his vision and the room came back into sharp focus. "Get a hold of yourself, man." Aiden shook his head from side to side then stood upright and poured himself another brandy and had yet another restorative sip.

Finally over whatever had happened to him, Aiden navigated the many obstacles in the room and went through the door. The night was closing in and he had expected to find the corridor in a twilight gloom but was surprised to see that all of the wall sconces had been lit. Telling himself that it must have been Mrs. Gittings, he wandered down the stairs, across the hall and out into the night.

♎☷☶♌

"I've told him to rest up for a few days," Doctor Lester began as they stood in the parlour of the stable house. "He's had one heck of a bang to the head. Can you cope without him for a week or so?"

"Certainly," Aiden replied emphatically. "I'm sure we can manage. I'll give Jack a hand with the horses. I don't mind rolling my sleeves up and helping out where necessary."

"Splendid. Though, if you don't mind me saying, you look a tad unwell yourself. Jack tells me that you had something of a dizzy spell?"

Aiden sighed and tried to put his recent experience into words...and failed. "It was nothing, really. Just the effects of exhaustion and too much brandy, I fear. I've been burning the candle at both ends for a while, I confess. I'm sure I'll be fine after a good night's sleep."

Lester clapped him on the shoulder. His grip was firm and gave Aiden a jolt. "Glad to hear it, dear boy. From what Jack said, it sounded like you were having an *episode* like poor Tom."

This piqued Aiden's interest and his brow furrowed. "Oh? Do go on."

"It was while Jack was over at the house getting you. Just after eight, I heard the clocks chime and he suddenly went distant and into a kind of fever state. His temperature rocketed and he started babbling about living flame and smokey tentacles!" Lester paused and studied Aiden's reaction; clearly, he had given something away. "I thought it was the effects of the laudanum I had given him, but hearing that you had a similar thing..."

"Well," Aiden had firmly reattached his mask of sanity. "That is damned odd. Just after eight, you say..." The numbers 22 flashed in front of his eyes as a realisation dawned. "Two minutes past eight...22..." he mumbled. Lester cocked his eyebrow as Aiden thought aloud. "It's on a twenty-four-hour clock. So, two-thousand-two is two minutes past eight. That would mean..."

At this point, Lester cut in. "I'm sorry? I confess to having no idea what you are blathering about, dear chap. Are you sure you are quite well?"

"Ugh! Yes, sorry. Just thinking aloud. It's just something I was reading in my uncle's notes."

"I see..." Lester said in the studied manner of a doctor that was well acquainted with the maladies of the human mind. "You don't want to be giving too much thought to your uncle's notes. The portion I saw was clearly the ravings of a disturbed mind. He became obsessed with numerology and 'mirror hours' before his death. An obsession that I am safe to say speeded his downfall. He was convinced that *something* was trying to communicate with him through symmetrical numbers and reflections. Clearly, his spectrophobia had bloomed out of all control."

Aiden shrugged to give the impression that his interest was nothing more than a passing curiosity. "Oh, I assure you that I don't believe a word of it. I'm just trying to make sense of what was wrong with him. As fantasies go, it is quite unique."

"Indeed. But I fear if you don't mind me saying, that trying to unravel the ravings of a madman is something of a grand folly that can only lead to disquiet. Phobias are something that man has puzzled over since he learned to walk upright."

"Spectrophobia." Aiden said flatly. "It seems such a strange word for a fear of mirrors, *spectro* brings to mind spooks and phantoms."

Lester smiled. "Indeed. In fact, spectrophobia can *also* mean a fear of spectral forms. It is the appearance of ghostly figures in mirrors and reflections that drives this particular phobia. The feeling that something is there when you catch a reflection out of the corner of your eye, that sort of thing."

"Fascinating. I must confess to finding the whole notion of phobias quite intriguing..."

Before Aiden could finish, Jack entered the room and gave a polite cough before speaking. "Beggin' yer pardon, sirs. Young Tom has come 'round and is askin' fer ye."

"Very well." Aiden nodded. "Thank you, Jack. We are on our way."

The stable house was a cramped two up, two down affair that had fallen into a state of decay. The proximity to the horses meant that the whole house smelt of dung. It was so pungent that it made Aiden's eyes water as he followed Jack up the creaking staircase and into Tom's sparsely furnished room.

"Hello, Tom." Aiden smiled. "Jack says that you wanted to see me?"

Tom shrugged. His eyes were glazed over and his speech slurred. "Yeah...though, I don't really know what to say. It's a feelin' I get, that's all."

"Don't trouble yourself, Tom," Lester interjected. "You need to rest."

Tom ignored him entirely and spoke directly to Aiden. "Something is coming...

something evil. I've felt it...heard it call to me. When I was out cold, it touched my mind... It burns!" Tom's voice suddenly rose to a yelp and panic flashed over his face.

Lester hurried around the bed and put his hand on Tom's chest. "Calm down, Tom. You've had a nasty blow to the head and it's disturbing your thoughts."

"No!" Tom barked in outrage. "It's real, I tell you." He looked pleadingly at Aiden. "You need to listen to me. You're in great danger. It wants your soul!"

Aiden was terrified by Tom's words. In his heart, he knew them to be the truth. He had felt *something* himself. "*What* does, Tom? *What* wants my soul?"

Tom's face was a mask of fear as he named the ancient evil that haunted Conley House. "Cthugha! The burning one is coming!" His warning delivered, Tom quickly fell into delirium brought on by his injury and Lester's laudanum. Aiden asked him to tell him everything he knew about Cthugha but it was no good, Tom fell through the layers of stupor and into a deep slumber.

"Jack, do you know what Tom was talking about?" Aiden looked into the furtive eyes of the old groundsman.

"I can't say as I do, sir. But..."

"Go on?"

"Well, it ain't my place to say, but Master Kenneth spoke of such things. Old ones, 'e called 'em. Said that they were wakin' up or summat. It was in those books of 'is. Them is evil books, sir. No good can come of reading 'em."

"Hmm." Aiden pondered for a moment before realising that he had seen the word Cthugha amongst the notes in his uncle's notebook. "Thank you, Jack. That's most helpful." He turned to Doctor Lester. "Did he ever say anything to you about these old ones? You said he had been raving of late?"

Lester shook his head. "He may have done. I don't recall. He was talking all manner of nonsense towards the end. I rarely gave anything he said a second thought." He stopped and fixed Aiden with a curious expression. "You can't believe this rubbish, surely?"

Aiden remained silent.

Lester continued, "Tom is delirious from his concussion and has imagined that some supernatural force is behind it. It's not uncommon for paranoia in such cases, as I'm sure you know. No doubt the poor lad has heard some superstitious twaddle from your uncle and has imagined it real. He should be fine after a good rest. You should get some too."

Aiden thought to argue that there may be something more to Tom's words than paranoid delusions but stopped himself. What good would it do? It was clear that Lester's mind was firmly closed to such ideas. Hell, his own mind had been closed to such things before that evening, but now...

"You're probably right." Aiden smiled at Lester. "I'll be heading back over to the house, then."

"Yes, go." Lester insisted. "I'll stay here with Tom, to keep an eye on him. I'll send Jack over if there is any trouble."

"Very well. Jack, would you see me out? Goodnight, Doctor Lester."

"Aye, sir. Follow me." Despite his years, Jack displayed a certain nimbleness as he navigated the crooked stairs. Aiden, however, struggled and nearly came a cropper. Jack led him through the parlour to the door. "Here ye go, sir. Don't worry about Tom, sir. I'll keep an eye on 'im."

"Thank you, Jack. I'm sure Doctor Lester has it under control."

Jack sniffed. He didn't say as much but Aiden could see in his eyes that he thought little of Lester's skills. "Aye. But still..."

Aiden paused in the doorway and asked Jack in hushed tones, "If Tom says anything else, could you write it down for me?"

Jack fidgeted uncomfortably. "I would, sir. Only, I can't write, see..."

"I'm sorry, Jack." Aiden felt his cheeks flush with colour. "Just remember it then."

"Certainly, sir." Jack beamed and tapped his temple with his forefinger. "The old noggin is still as solid as the foundations, sir. I'll remember."

"Thank you, Jack. Goodnight."

"Goodnight, sir." Jack pulled the door closed as he went back inside.

Aiden turned and started to walk back towards the house. As he did, a flicker of shadow passed the landing window. He stopped in his tracks and gazed upwards. There was nothing there now. Nothing except the flicker of one lonely candle in the sconce next to his bedroom door.

♀ℬℨℭℓ

"Twenty-two, 33, 55, 11." Aiden wrote the numbers in descending order down a sheet of blank notepaper. He placed them next to the corresponding words from the notes he found in the numerology book then turned his attention to the longer numbers on the chalkboard. "So, if we use the twenty-four-hour clock, then two minutes past eight is 22. Twelve minutes past nine is 33. Thirty-two minutes past eleven is 55, and ten past one is 11."

Once the numbers were laid out in some semblance of order, the whole thing started to make more sense. "So, just after eight, this *entity* had a hold of me. Ambition, accomplishment, depression and self-destruction..." He pondered the words for a minute. "Whose ambition? Mine or this...*Cthugha*?"

Placing his pen into the inkwell, Aiden started to leaf through the notebook for references to Cthugha. He didn't have to read far. "Here we are. '*The burning one from Fomalhaut, dread Cthugha can be summoned and bargained with but only under certain conditions. The Comte d'Erlette mentions* the burning reflection *on many occasions in the Cultes des Goules. After some study, I have come to believe that the only way to communicate with Cthugha is through the use of mirrors* at mirror hours, specifically symmetrical mirror hours.' Uncle, what have you done?"

Aiden flipped ahead before reading aloud another passage of his uncle's ramblings. "'*We are close to solving the mystery that has haunted me since childhood. Why have I always seen things in mirrors that others cannot? Why do I hear the whisperings from the gulfs of space? It seems the answer is that I have been chosen as an emissary for the burning god. We have studied Prinn, Goeterez, and Alhazred and have figured out how to summon Cthugha. G has been a great help in this matter...*'" Aiden's brow wrinkled in suspicion. "G? Gittings?" In his mind, this all but confirmed the housekeeper's complicity in the lunacy that plagued Conley House. "Damn her."

Ding!

As the clock struck nine, Aiden's heart hammered in panic. If there was any truth behind the notes and his uncle's calculations, Cthugha would make his presence felt in precisely twelve minutes. "Thirty-three... Communication and persuasion." There was no way in hell that he wanted to communicate with this *force from outside*, as his uncle had called it. Suddenly, his desire to uncover all the mirrors and windows in the house appeared rash.

There was no time to close all of the curtains and cover the mirrors so he contented himself with the study. After the curtains were drawn and with the velvet drape back on the mirror, he sat at the desk and watched the hands of the clock with a mounting terror. Just before twelve minutes past, Aiden blew out the candle and sat in the dark holding his breath and praying. Aiden counted every torturous second, anticipating *something*, but nothing happened. Not straight away, anyway.

As Aiden counted to 33, a piercing scream echoed from down the hall. Aiden jumped and knocked a pile of notes and old books to the floor. "Kirsten?" he called out as he groped around in the dark for the door. Finally locating it, he pulled the door open just as the candle on the desk burst into a blinding flame.

The heat from the flame was intense. Aiden shielded his face from it as he stepped back into the room and reached for the candlesnuffer on the mantlepiece. He had never seen a use for such an item before as a good puff of air usually sufficed. Something told him that this wasn't going to be so easily extinguished.

A core of molten orange radiated outwards into an intense yellow that burned with blue vapour trails that whipped above it like the fronds of an anemone.

"What do you want?" Aiden asked as he approached the flame.

The seething ball of fire seemed to hiss and tremble in an approximation of mirth. Aiden cried out in alarm as the velvet drape over the mirror ignited with a ferocious roar and was obliterated in seconds. With every passing moment, the flame swelled. It should have been impossible. The candle was merely an inch in thickness and the intense heat had rendered it down to a mere stub. Rivulets of molten red wax dripped from the table onto the floor where it soon solidified in thick pools.

Aiden looked at the flame, then looked at the snuffer in dismay. The tarnished silver tool was now dwarfed by the flame. In a moment of madness, Aiden pictured a child's drawing of the sun wearing a gnome's hat—that's what it would have been like. He tossed the cone-shaped item into the hearth in ignominy and looked around the room for something, anything, he could smother it with.

Finally, Aiden's eyes fell upon a metal wastepaper basket in the corner. He darted across the room and tipped out the balls of paper onto the floor. The bucket smelt charred, as though *someone* had used it for this very purpose before. With a smooth movement, Aiden brought the bucket down over the flame with a clang and held it flat against the desk.

Sweat poured from his brow and sizzled on the tin base of the bucket. The flame scorched the desk and threatened to melt the bucket. Aiden had to remove his jacket and wrap his hands in it to avoid them being seared like prime rump steak. Then, it suddenly went cold. Aiden grabbed his brandy and gulped down the lot. It hit his head much harder than he anticipated and he had to steady himself on the desk.

A repeat of the same blood-curdling scream snapped him out of his alcohol-induced fug. Using the flickering light from the open doorway, Aiden barreled across the room and out onto the landing. The flames on the candle sconces danced to a nonexistent rhythm, making the corridor shift, change shape, and flicker. It was a disturbing effect that made Aiden's guts lurch with every dip. It was the same kind of lighting effect that lighting men employed in the theatre productions of penny dreadful's that he had enjoyed as a boy but far more unsettling.

The flames were all of uniform size and shape, which should have been impossible. They also moved in perfect unison. It was as though they were being choreographed or manipulated on puppet strings. Aiden didn't have time to worry about them at that moment. The screams coming from Kirsten's room were gathering in hysteria— the young maid sounded like she was fighting for her life.

Bursting through the door, it came as a shock to find the room in total darkness except for the dim light from one small candle, that wouldn't have looked out of place on a birthday cake, reflected in Kirsten's dressing table mirror. Kirsten sat in front of the mirror, seemingly in a trance, wearing a pink nightie and a matching nightcap. Her mouth fell slack as he watched her reflection in the mirror and a keening wail came from deep inside of her. It was a mournful ululation that prompted the hairs on his arms to stand on end.

"Kirsten?" Aiden asked softly. "Kirsten, it's me, Aiden. Can you hear me?"

The maid didn't register his presence. There was not even the slightest flutter of an eyelid. It was then that he noticed that the girl's eyes were rolled back into her skull, showing two glistening white orbs.

Moving slowly to avoid startling her, Aiden approached her from behind and gently let one of his hands rest on her shoulder. "Kirsten...?"

"hup fm'latghor, Cthugha nafl'fhtagn!" Kirsten's mouth exploded with a guttural stream of syllables and her eyes suddenly became burning orange cinders. Her left hand shot up and grabbed Aiden's. Her grip was like iron as she dug her nails into his flesh, drawing blood.

Aiden winced. "Kirsten, stop!"

"Iä! Iä! Cthugha hup nog Fomalhaut!" Kirsten's fingers burned as the nails dug deeper and deeper into his hand. Steam was rising as the drawn blood was starting to boil. Aiden screamed.

"What the 'ell!" Jack burst into the room and stared in horror at Kirsten's eyes. The reflection of her burning eyes blended with the reflection of the small candle to make a grotesque amalgamation that looked like the hideously twisted visage of a demon from Hell.

Aiden screamed through gritted teeth as Kirsten continued to dig her nails into his hand. Jack ducked into the small washroom and grabbed the jug of well water next to the bowl. Without pause, he leapt across the room and flung the water over Kirsten.

The effect was instantaneous. As the water doused the candle and splashed into her eyes, her body went limp and her hand fell from Aiden's, leaving livid crescent shapes in his skin. Jack caught her as she slipped sideways off the stool and laid her down on the bed. "What the bloody 'ell is goin' on, sir?" he groaned with exertion.

"Thank you, Jack." Aiden winced as he wrapped his hand in his handkerchief. "I don't like to think what would have happened if you hadn't turned up."

"Aye, it's only by chance. I'd come over to tell ye that Tom was havin' another *fit*. It were just like the one what miss Kirsten were 'avin', 'is eyes were all rolled back in 'is 'ead and 'e were talkin' in tongues. What's goin' on, sir?"

"I'm afraid you'll think I'm mad, Jack," Aiden sighed. "I think that my uncle had been dabbling in the occult and has awoken some *force*..." He paused, awaiting a sceptical response. When Jack merely looked at him with understanding, he continued. "You don't look surprised. Why?"

"Well, sir...I don't like to speak ill of the dead or nowt, but yer uncle was a devilish kind of fellow. 'E were into all kinds of strange practices...'im and 'is *coven*."

"Coven?" Aiden's eyebrow cocked and his blood quickened.

"Aye, 'im and 'is cronies. I jus' thought it were folly, is all. Chantin' in the barn with numbers an' symbols chalked on the wall...that kinda thing. I asked 'im about it once and 'e told me that it were 'armless...sort of a prayer to bring good fortune. I didn't like it one bit, gimmie the willies, it did. But no good ever came o' pressin' 'im. It were best jus' to let it lie. Crazed 'e were, by the end. Mad as a March hare."

Aiden was going to ask him just *who* his uncle's cohorts had been but he was cut off by the abrasive tones of Mrs. Gittings who had materialised in the doorway. "Jack Angove!" she snapped. "I will not have you slandering Master Kenneth's good name!"

Gittings was dressed from head to toe in black. The flickering light in the corridor behind her made it appear that her head was bobbing on some kind of spectral wave. Aiden fixed her with an icy stare and levelled an accusing finger at her face, his eyes flashing with barely controlled rage. "You...you know all about this, don't you? Tell me how we can stop this, or God help me..."

"What's going on?" Kirsten squeaked, startling Aiden and Jack. "Why are you in my room and why is it so hot?"

"Calm down, Kirsten," Aiden purred. "You've just had a funny turn, that's all." He glanced at Jack, who returned his gaze knowingly. It was best not to go into the details at that moment. No good would come of upsetting her. "What do you remember?"

Kirsten had sat up on the bed and covered her face with her hands as though checking to see that her skin was intact. "Um...I was just getting ready for bed. I was sitting at the dresser and there was a flash. Then it got hot...so hot, and I must have had an attack of the vapours or something. Then I woke up. Why is it so hot?"

"Calm yourself, Kirsten. Everything's all right now. Open a window would you, Jack?" Aiden hid his hand as he spoke, not wanting to distress her any further.

"Aye, sir." Jack crossed the room and wrenched the old sash window open. It put up one hell of a fight but Jack won in the end. The cool, fresh night air gushed through the window. "There. Get a good lungful."

"Mrs. Gittings?" Aiden turned to ask her to fetch water but was greeted by an empty doorway. "Mrs. Gittings! Damn it, where has the blasted woman gone to now?"

"She left ages ago." Jack shrugged.

"Never mind, she can wait. Jack, could you fetch some water?" Aiden looked at Jack for a few seconds. He was miles away, just gazing out of the window at the cottage. "Jack...? Jack?!"

"Sorry, sir." His eyes never left the window as he spoke. "Something's wrong, I reckon."

Aiden moved over to the window. "What is it, Jack?"

"I'm sure I 'eard shouting, sir."

As they watched in stunned silence, the cottage window flared with light then burst outwards in a gout of flame. Shards of glass and splinters of wood radiated outwards and covered the yard like snow. Flames licked out of the window and caught the thatched roof. It went up in seconds. Kirsten screamed as the fire roared and spat. Fat columns of smoke thrashed in the air like tentacles above the building.

"My God!" Aiden gasped.

"Tom!" Jack bellowed and raced from the room. Aiden followed him, leaving Kirsten to sob quietly with her face buried in her hands.

♀℥℥♉

"Quick!" Aiden bellowed as they neared the blazing cottage. "Fetch water!" Jack grunted and took off towards the well. The fire had started on the upper floor and had quickly spread. Aiden ran to the door and pulled it open. Black smoke billowed out into the night.

"Tom?! Doctor Lester?!" he called into the smouldering parlour. Fire moved over the ceiling like a liquid, swirling and spreading, dancing with colour. Aiden covered his mouth and nose with the crook of his arm and entered the room. A jug of water stood on the table in the centre of the room. Using his free hand, he picked it up and doused the stairs with the water. "Doctor Lester? Can you hear me?"

"I'm here!" Lester's voice made Aiden jump and snap his head towards the door. Lester was holding a bucket of water and standing next to Jack. "Take this." He handed Aiden the bucket.

"Where the hell were you?" Aiden barked as he tipped the contents of the bucket onto the fire that was creeping down the stairs.

"I'd popped outside for some fresh air. Tom had passed out again after Jack went to get you. Then the window exploded. I ran to fetch water, that's when I bumped into Jack."

"Bumped is right, you nearly knocked me on my arse," Jack grunted indignantly as he passed Aiden the next bucket.

Before he could use it, the ceiling began to creak and rumble. "Out!" Lester screamed and grabbed Aiden by the shoulders, dragging him from the building. Seconds later, the ceiling gave way and crashed to the floor. A metal-framed bed came with it. Upon the bed was the evident source of the blaze: a gigantic cinder in the shape of a human being. The heat was intense and roared as it tasted the fresh oxygen.

"Back! Get away from there, the whole building's coming down," Aiden screamed and dragged his two cohorts away from the cottage. They made it to safety not a moment too soon. The framework of the building gave way and it collapsed in upon itself in a shower of dust and sparks. The noise was deafening as timbers cracked and stone shattered.

"Fetch help from the village!" Aiden instructed.

"No use, sir, they won't come." Jack said in a matter-of-fact manner, as though it was a given.

"What?" Aiden exploded. "Why the hell not?"

"He's right," Lester explained. "People around here won't come within a hundred yards of the place. They say the place is cursed."

"I'm starting to think they're right," Aiden admitted. "Fine, fetch the buckets, we'll have to take care of the blaze ourselves. We can't let it spread to the stables."

For more than an hour, they fought the savage fire. Kirsten had joined them and they had created a loose-linked chain to the well. Once it was contained, Jack and Aiden smothered the flames with manure and compost. The stench that pervaded the winding streets of Hollowhills was overpowering yet not one single soul offered their assistance. It seemed that Jack was correct in his assertion that the village gave Conley House a very wide berth indeed.

It was just before eleven o'clock when they decided it was safe to leave the ruins of the stable house. It was now little more than a gutted shell, a smouldering pile of charred rubble. And, somewhere amongst the wreckage, lay the remains of Tom the stable boy. Kirsten wept. She had been fond of Tom; she had often hoped that he would ask her to elope with him but, alas, that never transpired. Now it never would.

Aiden collapsed on the grass next to the well in a numbed state of shock. Despite his attempts to block the manifestation of Cthugha, the malign force from outside had managed to break through in more drastic ways than he would ever have imagined. First, Kirsten had been, seemingly, possessed, then Tom.

Doctor Lester paced agitatedly around the well while Jack shot filthy looks in his direction. The odd-job-man blamed Lester for leaving Tom alone. He mused that if he hadn't, then he would have been able to douse the flames before they raged out of control. Lester believed that Tom must have knocked the candle onto his bedsheets during his fever. Aiden and Jack knew better, but Lester stubbornly refused to believe them, leading to a tense moment between the two doctors. Lester was convinced that Aiden was suffering some malady of the mind, probably brought on by immersing himself in his uncle's work. After all, madness did indeed run in his family.

Jack left his perch on the low stone wall that lined the boundary of the garden revealing the expanse of Bodmin Moor beyond and walked over to Kirsten. He gently put his hand on her shoulder to comfort her. Aiden smiled at Jack; the man had a tender soul underneath his rough exterior. "You can have my room tonight, Jack." Aiden smiled. "We'll see about sorting you out a permanent room on the morrow." Not that he was going to say as much, but he had plans that would leave a room vacant very soon; remembering this made him suddenly realise that *someone* was conspicuous by her absence.

"Where the hell is that damn woman, Gittings?" Aiden snarled. "She didn't lift a finger to help."

"Dunno, sir. I ain't seen 'er since we were in Kirsten's room," Jack replied.

Aiden rose and straightened his attire. It was about time that he confronted Mrs. Gittings and put an end to *whatever* was going on. He looked up and saw a shadow looking down upon them from the landing window, it was backlit by the unearthly flicker from the candles. His fists clenched tightly as he scowled up at the dim figure. "I'm just going to have a word with my housekeeper."

As he stalked towards the house, Jack caught up with him. "Go easy on 'er, sir. She means well, she just misses master Kenneth, that's all."

"I wish I could believe that, Jack, I really do."

♀ℇȝ♋⅄

Aiden entered Conley Manor and shut the door behind him. A trio of flickering candles danced on the low table next to the stairs. The light it cast stretched up the walls like fingers. The air was thick and hot, settling on his skin and clogging his pores. He was about to mount the staircase when he heard a deafening crash from the drawing room. He grabbed the door handle and swung the door open.

"Mrs. Gittings!" he cried out in anger as he saw his housekeeper with a hammer in one hand and a pool of mirror shards around her feet. "What the hell do you think you are doing?"

"Saving us all!" she screamed hysterically as she dragged the curtains closed. "We were safe until *you* opened the curtains and uncovered the mirrors. It's all your fault!" She levelled an accusatory finger at him and bared her twisted yellow teeth.

"My fault?" Aiden scoffed. "This is all your doing, you and my lunatic uncle. You brought that *thing* here."

Mrs. Gittings gasped in outrage. "*My* doing? I had nothing to do with this. It is you and *your* cursed bloodline that is at fault here. You're the ones to blame!"

Aiden had never been tempted to strike a woman before, but the venom in her voice brought his anger bubbling to the surface. He gritted his teeth and shoved his hands deep into his pockets to avoid the temptation.

"There is no point in denying your involvement, you evil old crone. I found the notes in the diary about G. You're the only G that I know. I bet those scribbles that aren't in his hand match up with yours perfectly."

Her mouth opened and closed like a fish gasping for water. "I have no idea what you are talking about." Her voice betrayed a thinly veiled rage that seemed to spread through her wiry frame. Her eyes took on a harder edge and started to twinkle like embers.

"Rubbish!" Aiden spat. "It was you that frightened Tom half to death wasn't it? He saw you in the window, didn't he?"

Gittings' body trembled and shook. Her mouth opened into a vulturous rictus.

"Confess, damn you. Confess!"

Every shard of the mirror around Mrs. Gittings' feet lit with flame reflected from the candles on the sideboard. Her eyes flared and smoke billowed from her mouth. *"Cthugha, Fhtagn!"*

Aiden bellowed in horror as she became a solid column of flame. Grabbing the vase of freshly cut flowers off the table and praying that they had been watered that afternoon, he tossed the flowers aside and pitched the water over her. It sizzled and turned to steam in an instant.

Gittings took two steps in his direction with her hands outstretched and then dropped like a stone. Her body covered the mirror shards and the blaze snuffed itself out. The smell of burning housekeeper was too much for Aiden. He barged through the door, out of the front door, then vomited in a pot of petunias.

"Jack! Doctor Lester!" he cried out between retches. "For the love of God!"

Nobody answered.

Aiden tottered around the corner with his hand over his mouth. There was nobody in sight. He hadn't heard them go in after him so he assumed that they would still be around the well.

"Kirsten...? Jack...?"

He took two hesitant steps away from the wall and was startled by a scuffling noise from behind. "Jack?"

Thunk!

Something hard and heavy connected with the back of his head and everything went black.

⚥℞ᚖᚑ

The pungent aroma of smelling salts scythed up Aiden's nostrils. Flashes of colour popped on the insides of his eyelids as consciousness came flooding back to him.

"Come on, Aiden. Wake up, there's a good chap. We can't have you late for the party, can we?"

As his eyes cleared, he was greatly taken aback to be greeted with the smugly grinning face of Doctor Lester.

"Lester? Wh-what the..." Aiden spluttered. As he raised his head, he became aware of the fact that his hands were bound to a wooden beam. He was in the barn. The floor had been cleared and he was positioned in the centre of a chalk ring embellished with numbers and occult symbols. Circling him was a perfect circle of mirrors that Lester had removed from their frames.

"Don't try to talk. You've been out for some time. I'm afraid I hit you harder than I planned." Lester hefted a piece of timber in his free hand. The end was thick with clotted blood and tufts of straggly white hair. "Not as hard as I hit Jack, though." A sick grin spread from ear to ear. "I'm afraid he won't be joining us."

"You bastard!" Aiden spat. Anger cleared his cobwebs and returned strength to his body as the acrid taste of adrenaline burned the back of his throat. "What have you done with Kirsten?"

Lester pointed to a darkened corner where a figure sat tied to a chair. "She's alive...for now. These sorts of things always demand a sacrifice, you know?"

"Let her go, you bounder, or I'll—"

"You'll do nothing!" Lester screamed in his face. He took a strange ceremonial dagger with a wavy blade out of his leather medical bag and waved it under Aiden's nose. "If I didn't need your body for the master, I'd slit your throat right now. Sadly, your body is to be the vessel, so I can't have my fun."

Aiden's head throbbed and his chest was tight. "Why?" was all he could manage to ask.

"Still hasn't sunk in, has it?" Lester smiled. "You Conley's never were the smartest bunch. I've been waiting my whole life to free my lord, Cthugha, from his exile. We Lesters were born into the sacred order of the flame and have spent generations cultivating your miserable bloodline. You were born for this moment, all of you were. Conley, you see, means 'purifying flame.' We thought that Kenneth was the one. His name meant 'fire born' and I wasted my whole damn life trying to get him to embrace Cthugha! Sadly, his heart gave out as we attempted the summoning. I guess that means that the honour of feeling Cthugha's flame falls to you, 'little fire.'"

"You're mad!" Aiden winced as he struggled against his bonds.

"Not so. I'm blessed. It will be I that frees Cthugha. You see, when I figured out the mirror hours and got your uncle to look into the numerology, I realised the importance of the number 11. Betrayal, dear boy." Lester cackled like a madman. "Betrayal is essential. Only through the purity of hate can Cthugha be freed. Hence this whole charade; it was necessary to get you ready. You do hate me, don't you?"

"You sick, crazy, son of a whore."

"Good, good. You're perfectly primed for the purity of flame." Lester looked at his fob-watch. "Seven minutes past one, three minutes to go."

"What part did that shrew, Gittings play in this?" Aiden asked in a desperate attempt to distract him from his preparations.

Lester tipped his head back and roared with laughter. "None whatsoever. She was entirely innocent."

"But, the G in the notes..."

Stopping and holding out his hand in greeting, Lester grinned. "Granville Thomas Lester at your service. I don't tend to use my Christian name outside of order business."

Aiden struggled harder as Doctor Lester lit the candles that were positioned around his legs between the mirrors. Next, Lester positioned a chair in front of Aiden. On it was a semi-circular object covered in a moth-eaten velvet cloth. It was the mirror from the study.

"It's time," Lester crowed and uncovered the mirror. "Come, Cthugha. Your time is at hand!"

The candle flames stretched and elongated with a mighty rush. The flames left the wicks and hovered in churning balls over the six mirrors at Aiden's feet.

"Iä! Iä! Cthugha! Fhtagn!"

The flames grew and danced as wispy tendrils of fire stretched out from their bodies. The flames finally touched each other and spread into a perfectly circular hoop around Aiden's head.

Intense heat singed Aiden's hair as he

screamed in pain. He could feel his forehead blistering, feel the sweat boiling and sizzling. "No!"

With a whoosh, the flames left the mirrors and formed itself into a gigantic globe that hung in front of his face. It drifted back slightly until it was perfectly lined up with the mirror on the chair.

"Open your eyes, let him in!" Lester demanded.

"Never!" Aiden vowed through gritted teeth. He knew that if he opened his eyes, he was a goner.

Lester cursed and stepped into the circle with the blade in his hand. "If you won't open them, then I'll slice your blasted eyelids off!"

The evil doctor was inches from Aiden when...

"No, ye won't, ye mad bugger!" Jack charged from the shadows and impaled Lester on a rusty pitchfork.

"No!" Lester screamed as he pitched backwards and crashed into the mirror on the chair.

The ball of flame that was Cthugha hissed furiously as the connection was broken. Jack stumbled unsteadily, clutching a livid gash on his forehead. He grabbed the knife from the floor where it had fallen and cut Aiden's bonds.

"Thank you, Jack," Aiden panted. "I thought you were dead."

Jack smiled a crooked smile. "Nay, sir. We Angove's have thick skulls, an' 'e's got less punch than one of farmer Ashcroft's sheep."

A burst of manic laughter halted the bonhomie. "You fools!" Lester spat a gobbet of black blood from his mouth. The pitchfork was impaled in his abdomen and stuck straight up in the air like a flagpole. "It's too late...Cthugha comes!"

Lester raised the study mirror over his head and cackled as the swirling mass of flame spun and vibrated.

"What do we do, sir," Jack asked as the conflagration grew.

Aiden thought for a minute. The evil fiery orb had grown to the size of a beach ball. It crackled and spat as it rippled in a kaleidoscope of oranges, reds, and yellows. Before he could reply, the mass shuddered and hundreds of glistening black eyes burst open and glared at them hatefully. Thick tentacles sprouted from its bulk and snapped in their direction. Aiden pushed Jack out of harm's way. "Get

Kirsten, and get the hell out of here!" he bellowed as a flaming appendage coiled around his wrist.

Aiden screamed as the fire seared his skin. More of the tentacles swarmed over doctor Lester and consumed him. The mirror fell and for a second, Cthugha's strength faltered. The tentacles released Aiden from their grasp as the Burning One became less solid, somehow blurrier. Aiden knew this might be his last chance to banish the malignant deity and he had to act.

Dashing forwards, Aiden grabbed the mirror with his bare hands. The pain was intense but he had no other option. Picking up the mirror, he fled from the barn. Cthugha swirled in the air as Aiden raced towards the well. A tentacle cracked like a whip from the awful bulk and coiled around Aiden's neck. He screamed as the fire entered his ears...then everything became numb and he was falling. Cthugha hissed in rage one last time as Aiden and the mirror plunged into the icy waters at the bottom of the well.

Aiden's twisted remains were later recovered from the well, his fingers fused to the mirror. The last of the Conley line was no more. Jack had been cunning and had placed the remains of Lester and Gittings amongst the still-smouldering wreckage of the cottage and erased all traces of ritual from the barn. He knew that nobody would believe the truth, so he and Kirsten decided it was for the best to let it be known that Tom, Lester and Gittings had perished in the cottage fire and that Aiden had tragically died whilst attempting rescue. Thus earning him the hero's burial he deserved.

Once the funerals had been concluded, Kirsten took her meagre belongings and left Hollowhills. She had no trouble finding employment and landed a position as a maid to the Lexington-Brown's over at Chycoose Manor near High Bend. She never spoke of what happened on that awful night. Jack moved also, to the town of Betyls Cove where he took the position of verger to the local vicarage.

Conley House stood empty for decades. As nobody claimed it as inheritance, the ownership passed to the local parish. None of the villagers would go near the place and it fell into disrepair until it was purchased by a wealthy businessman in the Thirties. It was completely renovated and turned into a guest house. It still stands to this day and does a roaring trade on the back of the alleged "Beast of Bodmin" that is said to roam the area.

Some guests have commented over the years about the heat of the rooms. Some said that they felt inexplicably lightheaded or faint. All of the building's lights are now electric and nothing more serious than night sweats has occurred. The use of candles in the rooms is strictly forbidden.

Thanks for reading "Burning Reflection," a Mannison Minibook by Tim Mendees.

We hope you enjoyed the story! Please remember to leave a review at your favorite retailer.

This book is also available in ebook format.

To discover more Mannison Minibooks or learn about other Mannison Press publications, please visit the publisher's website at www.MannisonPress.com.

About the Author: Tim Mendees

Tim Mendees is a horror writer from Macclesfield in the North-West of England that specializes in cosmic horror and weird fiction. He has had over fifty stories accepted for publication in anthologies and magazines with publishers all over the world. When he is not arguing with the spellchecker, Tim is a goth DJ, crustacean and cephalopod enthusiast, and the presenter of a popular web series of live video readings of his material. He currently lives in Brighton & Hove with his pet crab, Gerald, and an army of stuffed octopods.

 www.timmendeeswriter.wordpress.com
 www.tinyurl.com/timmendeesyoutube
 facebook.com/goatinthemachine

Printed in Great Britain
by Amazon

67184947R00057